Chen Ping and His Magic Axe

DODD, MEAD & COMPANY
NEW YORK

Chen Ping and His Magic Axe

DEMI

For Sister Magdalen Mary, I.H.M.,

my teacher,
who always knew
who was what,
what was whose,
and what was what.

Book design by Barbara DuPree Knowles

1 2 3 4 5 6 7 8 9 10

Library of Congress Cataloging-in-Publication Data

Demi.
    Chen Ping and his magic axe.

    Summary: Chen Ping's honesty in his encounter
with a stranger causes his ax to acquire magic
powers, while his greedy master's attempt to reap
the same reward comes to a different end.
    [1. Folklore—China] I. Title.
PZ8.1.D38Ch 1987   398.2′1′0951 [E]   86-16655
ISBN 0-396-08907-0

Once there was a poor little boy named Chen Ping who worked for a rich man named Wing Fat. Chen Ping fetched water, cut firewood, and milled rice. He also took loving care of all the animals. But Wing Fat was never satisfied.

One bitterly cold day, Chen Ping
was sent out to collect firewood in
the mountains. He carried his axe
and a pole across his shoulder.

While crossing a narrow wooden
bridge, his axe fell down into the
river below. How could he chop wood
without his axe? Chen Ping
sat down on a rock and cried.

All of a sudden an old man with
a long white beard appeared,
followed by many wondrous animals.
"Why are you crying, my boy?"
the old man asked.

"Oh, sir! My axe has fallen into the river and I will be whipped by my master because I will have no firewood for him," said Chen Ping, wiping away his tears.

"Don't cry anymore," replied the old man. "I will bring it back for you."
So saying, the old man jumped into the river and came up with an axe.
"Is this your axe?" the old man asked.

Chen Ping looked at it very hard. It was wrought in solid silver
and glistened in the sunlight. But he shook his head and said,
"No, sir, that is not my axe."

The old man dove into the river again and came up with a different axe.
This one was finely crafted in shining gold and dazzled in the sunlight.
But Chen Ping shook his head and said, "That is not mine, either."

Smiling broadly, the old man dove down
once again and brought up Chen Ping's axe.
"Yes! Yes! *That* is my axe!" Chen Ping cried.
"Thank you so much, sir."

"Because you are such an honest boy," the old man said, "good luck
will always be yours. And do not be surprised," he added,
"if you find your axe to be much more of a treasure than the others."
With that, the old man disappeared as suddenly as he had come.
Chen Ping was amazed.

Then the boy remembered the chores he had to do for Wing Fat and ran up the mountain. In no time at all, and with very little effort from Chen Ping, the axe had chopped a full load of firewood. It was just like magic!

When Chen Ping came home, Wing Fat was ready to
scold him. But Chen Ping was so excited that he
burst out with the whole story of his adventure
and the wonders of the magic axe.

Chen Ping's story gave Wing Fat an idea. Early next morning, he picked up an old broken axe and headed up the mountain as if to collect firewood himself. When he reached the bridge he deliberately threw the axe into the river, sat down on a rock, and cried as loudly as possible.

Sure enough, the old man appeared before him and asked, "Why are you weeping?"

"Oh," sobbed Wing Fat. "My axe has fallen in the river and I'm sure I will be whipped."

"Do not cry anymore," said the old man. He dove into the river and immediately came up with the old broken axe.

"Oh, no!" cried Wing Fat, taken aback. "My axe is *far* more splendid than that one."

Again, the old man dove down and came up with the silver axe.
"Oh, no!" cried Wing Fat. "Mine was made of solid gold!"

The old man dove down again and
came up with the brilliant golden axe.
"My axe! My axe!" cried Wing Fat,
as he reached out and grabbed it
from the old man's hands.

Wing Fat was thinking of all the things he would buy
from the sale of the golden axe. He was so happy when he
came to the narrow wooden bridge that he jumped up and
down for joy. But he was so fat that the ropes snapped
and he fell down into the river below. Since that day,
no one has ever seen Wing Fat again.

And what about Chen Ping? His magic axe chopped so much wood, all by itself,
that Chen Ping was able to supply all the villagers with firewood,
take care of his beloved animals, and live happily ever after.

The Chinese dragon represents wealth, wisdom, and power, but he rarely reveals himself and therefore he survives. He hides in the mists and in the depths of rushing waters. He is wise and therefore he is quiet, he is powerful and therefore he is fast-moving, he is generous and therefore he is rich. When he is disturbed by human greed, the rivers and seas are lashed into huge waves, the earth shudders and evil men fall.

With his beautiful and virtuous partner, the Chinese phoenix, the universe maintains its heavenly order and reason prevails.

12 PEACHTREE

J
Picture   Demi.
          Chen Ping and his magic axe / Demi.
       -- New York : Dodd, Mead, c1987.
          [32] p. : col. ill. ; 22 cm.
          Summary: Chen Ping's honesty in his
       encounter with a stranger causes his ax
       to acquire magic powers, while his
       greedy master's attempt to reap the
       same reward comes to a different end.
          ISBN 0-396-08907-0

       R00461 83430   MAR 0 2 1988

          1. Folk tales, Chinese--Juvenile
       litrature. 2. China--Folklore--
       Juvenile literature.   I. Title

GA   11 DEC 87   13861587   GAPApc   86-16655